S0-BZT-328

FOR MUM

Monika and Luka:
Don't worry, be happy!

DON'T WORRY, DOUGLAS!

BY DAVID MELLING

SCHOLASTIC INC.
New York Toronto London Auckland
Sydney Mexico City New Delhi Hong Kong

Douglas and his dad were playing.
"What have you got behind your back?"
asked Douglas.
"Nothing," said Dad.
"Not that hand,
the other one!"
Dad smiled.
"Close your eyes. . . ."

"Wow!" said Douglas.
"Thanks, Dad!"
Douglas had never
had a woolly
hat before.
He couldn't wait
to show his friends.

"Take care of it," said Dad.

But Douglas was already off!

"Look at me!" Douglas cried.

"Snazzy hat, Douglas!"
baaed the sheep.

"I can even do cartwheels in it!" he whooped.
And he did. Again. And again.

Until something didn't feel right.

Douglas gasped. His new woolly hat had turned into one long string of spaghetti.

"That's not supposed to happen!" he said.
"Don't worry, Douglas," said the sheep.
"We'll fix it."
They wound it into a ball and squished it
back into shape.

"Any better?" they asked.
"NO!" said Douglas.

"Cow is a good
thinker," said
the sheep.
"She'll know
what to do."

Cow thought she had a *very* good idea.
"Pretty!" she said.

"**NO!**" said Douglas.

"Don't worry, Douglas," chirped a swoopy bird.
"I can use this for my nest."

"NO, YOU CAN'T!"
yelped Douglas.
"That's my new woolly hat!"

"Doesn't *look* like a woolly hat,"
said the swoopy bird.
"Anyway," she puffed,
"it doesn't fit!"
And she dropped it.

Just then, it began to rain and everyone hurried for cover. Except Douglas. "What's my dad going to say?" he worried.

Rabbit popped up. "Ooh, thanks, Douglas!
Just what I need to plug the hole in my burrow."
"THAT'S MY NEW WOOLLY HAT!"
cried Douglas. "Dad gave it to me."

"Sorry," said Rabbit, "I didn't know.
Come here," she said and wiped his nose.

"What am I going to do?" sniffed Douglas.

Rabbit looked thoughtful.

"Why don't you just tell him what happened?
He's nice, your dad. He'll understand."

Maybe Rabbit was right. Douglas picked up
his wet spaghetti hat and trudged back home.

"Oh, Douglas," said his mom.
"Look at you!"

"Where's your new hat?"
asked his dad.

Douglas told them
everything.

"Don't worry, Douglas," said Dad.

"I've got something for you. Guess which hand?"

Douglas wasn't sure.

"Here's *my* hat," said Dad, laughing.

"You'll soon grow into it!"

Banana Hat

Diaper Hat

I Don't Like Peas Hat

Follow-the-Leader Hat

Spot-the-Difference Hat

Best Friends Hat

Pants Hat

Peek-a-Boo Hat

Wig Hat

Weather Hat

Love Hat

Potty Hat

Family Hat